WITHDRAWN

KiD SQUAD

SAVES THE WORLD

The Battle of the Bots

by John Perritano   Illustrated by Mike Laughead

Calico

An Imprint of Magic Wagon
www.abdopublishing.com

www.abdopublishing.com

Published by Magic Wagon, a division of ABDO, PO Box 398166, Minneapolis, Minnesota 55439. Copyright © 2015 by Abdo Consulting Group, Inc. International copyrights reserved in all countries. No part of this book may be reproduced in any form without written permission from the publisher. Calico™ is a trademark and logo of Magic Wagon.

Printed in the United States of America, North Mankato, Minnesota.
062014
092014

Written by John Perritano
Illustrated by Mike Laughead
Edited by Rochelle Baltzer and Megan M. Gunderson
Cover and interior design by Candice Keimig

Library of Congress Cataloging-in-Publication Data

Perritano, John, author.
  The battle of the bots / by John Perritano ; illustrated by Mike Laughead.
      pages cm. -- (Kid Squad saves the world)
  Summary: Under orders, Colonel Bragg hires two companies to build the world's first robotic armies--but when the two robot leaders, Caesar and Napoleon, start thinking independently and fighting with real weapons it is up to the Kid Squad to save the world from Project Battle Bot.
  ISBN 978-1-62402-037-7
1. Robots--Juvenile fiction. 2. Battles--Juvenile fiction. 3. Inventions--Juvenile fiction. 4. Heroes--Juvenile fiction. [1. Robots--Fiction. 2. War--Fiction. 3. Inventions--Fiction. 4. Heroes--Fiction.] I. Laughead, Mike, illustrator. II. Title.
  PZ7.P43415Bat 2014
  813.6--dc23
                    2014012212

Table of **Contents**

Chapter 1
Jungle Fever

Simon Higgenbottom put the binoculars to his eyes. He looked out on the thick, damp jungle of an uncharted island in the South Pacific. Sweat rolled down his forehead and collected under his arms.

Standing to his right was Audrey Cambridge. She too was looking at the vast rain forest. The sunlight gleamed off her blonde hair.

The pair did not speak.

They never did.

They hated each other.

Colonel Ulysses T. Bragg walked over, gulped, and shook their sweaty hands. He had been dreading this day for a month. *I'm not very good at babysitting corporate types*, he thought.

"Exciting day," Bragg lied, knowing the history of ill will between the two. "I welcome you both."

"It is a great day, colonel," Higgenbottom said. "It's a great day for America. A bit hot, but still a great day."

"Indeed," echoed Cambridge. "For all of humankind for that matter. Peace may finally get a chance once I get the contract."

"What do you mean once *you* get the contract?" Higgenbottom blared. "No decision has been made yet. My product is vastly superior to yours."

"We shall see," Cambridge said in a mocking tone. "You haven't created anything worthwhile in years."

"Please, please, Mr. Higgenbottom, Ms. Cambridge," Bragg said, trying to quell the tension before an argument began. "It's too hot to argue. No decision has been made. That's why we're here today."

Colonel Bragg was not much of a diplomat. He felt more comfortable firing his mouth off first and apologizing later, which he often did. He was brusque, arrogant, and stubborn. Still, no one ever questioned his loyalty or patriotism.

President Novak had ordered Bragg to be on his best behavior. Project Battle Bot was not a done deal. Today's mock battle would go a long way in deciding which company was to create the world's first all-robotic army.

"I don't have to tell you that today's mock battle is top secret, as is this island," Bragg said. "It's one of several bases run by my Special Projects Division. It's a testing ground for new weapons, although we use it for other things."

"Like zee company picnics."

All eyes turned to the smiling figure standing behind Colonel Bragg. The man was scruffy. Despite the tropical heat, he wore a white lab coat stained with yesterday morning's blueberry pancakes. Seldom did this strange-looking man venture from his laboratory in the Amazon rain forest. Today, though, was a special occasion.

"May I present Dr. Ignatius Newton Stein," Bragg continued. "He'll be observing our mock battle today. He will report his observations to the president."

Higgenbottom and Cambridge extended their hands in the good doctor's direction. Dr. I.N. Stein wasn't prim, nor was he proper. He was, however, a good sport about many things and probably the smartest person on the planet.

Dr. Stein's trademark was his unkempt appearance. Standing 5 feet 9 inches tall, the professor's shoulders drooped slightly, as did most of his body. His wire-rimmed glasses tilted cockeyed at the end of his nose. His crazy hair was aflutter today as a warm breeze cascaded from the hills.

"Pleased to meet you, doctor," Cambridge said, shaking Dr. Stein's hand. "It is an honor. Your early work in robotic brain technology is the reason we are here today."

"Zee honor is mine," Dr. Stein said. "I've heard so much about you and zee androids. You have taken zee technology of robotic brains and given your robots a sense of humanity, no?"

"To some degree, although we are a long way from where we want to be," Cambridge said.

Feeling left out, Higgenbottom loudly cleared his throat.

"It is a pleasure to meet you, Dr. Stein," he said.

"Ah, no need for formalities," Dr. Stein said in his thick German accent. "Please call me Ignatius."

With all the pleasantries out of the way, Colonel Bragg ushered everyone near a spot on the ground marked with a concrete X. He pressed a button on his satellite phone. Within seconds, the area around the X opened like a trapdoor. An elevator rose from the opening.

"If everyone will follow me, we will take the elevator down thirteen flights to a special bunker-like control room," Colonel Bragg said in an uncharacteristically charming manner. "There, we can watch and study the simulation."

His guests eagerly stepped into the elevator. They were mesmerized at what they saw when they arrived below ground.

A huge air-conditioned room had been carved into the volcanic rock of the island. It was staffed with thirty members of Bragg's Special Projects Division. The room was crammed with video monitors, computers, and satellite imagery. A huge video map of the island dominated one wall.

"This is amazing," Higgenbottom said. "We have nothing like it at Electrocycle Industries."

"That's because you run a shoddy operation," Cambridge jabbed.

"Ms. Cambridge, Mr. Higgenbottom," Bragg said with a scowl, "I think it's time we briefed Dr. Stein on what we will be doing today. Please, everyone have a seat."

Everyone did as Bragg asked, each taking a seat around an oblong table in the center of the control room. Bragg sat at the far end.

"Dr. Stein," Bragg began, "as you know, the government has been working closely with Mr. Higgenbottom at Electrocycle Industries and Ms. Cambridge at Omni-Tech. We are developing the next generation of warriors . . ."

"Zee robots?" Dr. Stein interrupted.

"Yes, the robots," Bragg said. "While we have been using robots in one form or another for many years . . ."

"Like zee drones that fly like birds?" asked Dr. Stein.

"Yes, like zee, um, the, flying drones," Bragg answered, a bit annoyed. "As I was saying, we have been using robots in one form or another for years. Now we have taken it to the next level by creating robotic soldiers armed with the latest weapons.

"Each of the robots we will observe today has an amazingly sophisticated brain the likes of which we have never seen before. Their control centers have been programmed to not only reach a military objective, but also to understand, evaluate, and react better than a human would in the same situation."

Bragg stopped and sipped from a bottle of water. Dr. Stein reached into his pocket and pulled out a foil package. It was a triple-decker bologna, lettuce, tomato, banana, and mustard sandwich.

"Zee most tasty treat, no?" Dr. Stein said.

Everyone stared at him as he pulled apart the foil. The sound was like fingernails on a chalkboard.

"I'm so sorry," Dr. Stein said. "I did not eat a thing this morning. This is my favorite sandwich. Please continue, colonel," Dr. Stein added as he took a bite.

Bragg glared.

"The lead robots in each army—the generals—have the most powerful and complex brains," Bragg continued. "The privates have the least complex brains. Colonels are smarter than majors and captains, captains are smarter than lieutenants, and so on. The idea is to create an army that never questions orders."

"And follows zee general blindly?" Dr. Stein mumbled through mustard-covered lips.

He swallowed.

"History is full of stories of zee soldiers who follow their leaders blindly to no good end."

Bragg scowled and continued his lecture.

"Today, both Mr. Higgenbottom and Ms. Cambridge have flown in their robots from the United States. We will see a simulated war game to determine whose robot army is better—the army created by Electrocycle or the army created by Omni-Tech. Each company has designed its own robotic weapons and soldiers. They will fight one another, and we will judge their performance."

"I'm not so sure about zee robots becoming soldiers," Dr. Stein warned. "Soldiers need to be able to think on their feet, to think for themselves. They need to assess, how do you say, a *situation* and overcome zee obstacles. They need to have zee compassion and zee intelligence to act on their own. They need to know when not to pull zee trigger. They cannot just be killing machines, no. I am not so sure about zee Project Battle Bot."

Cambridge and Higgenbottom sat silent as Dr. Stein voiced his concerns. Cambridge spoke first.

"Unlike other robots, Dr. Stein, our bots are intuitive, even the private," she said. "In other words, they learn from each other and each situation. While they carry out their orders with detachment and objectivity, they are always learning. They see advantages and disadvantages in each situation. Their goal is to reach their objective. They can overcome. They can adapt. They can think. They can . . ."

"Exactly," Higgenbottom interrupted. "I don't always agree with Ms. Cambridge. In fact, I never agree with her. But, our robots are a state-of-the-art, mega-fighting force that no human army can destroy. And that is why this project is so important. That's why . . ."

Not one to let Higgenbottom have the last word, Cambridge interrupted.

"When others see how strong our robot army is, they will never wage war against us out of fear of being destroyed," she said. "We'll never have to use these robots in combat. Never. Peace will finally be achieved."

"Until zee enemies develop their own robotic armies," Dr. Stein said.

"And then it will be just like in the Cold War," Cambridge continued. "We had nuclear bombs and our enemies had nuclear bombs. No one used them because to do so would have meant the end of the world."

"MAD, they called it," Dr. Stein bellowed, his face now flushed. Bits of bologna, banana, and bread shot out of his mouth. "Mutual assured destruction. I know zee concept all too well, but you are much too young to know. I was in Berlin when zee Berlin Wall went up and divided zee city into East and West—communists and those who wanted to be free. We came close to using zee bombs many times by accident. It is no way to live."

"That's what's so great about our robotic army," Higgenbottom said. "They're too smart to make mistakes."

Chapter 2
Hail Caesar

The sun blazed high in the sky when the war games began. On one side was the Blue Army. It was led by a robotic general the scientists at Electrocycle Industries nicknamed Caesar. They took the name from the ruthless Roman dictator.

Caesar was a G7 robot. Higgenbottom believed it was the most imposing robot on the island. He was more than right. Gigantic in stature, Caesar and the robots under its command were machine-like. The head of each robot was painted a different color depending on its rank. Caesar's head was painted gold—the color of a leader.

Despite their bulky frames, the bots were quick and agile. Their control centers, or brains, were sophisticated, particularly Caesar's. It could process millions of bits of information in seconds. Caesar saw cracks in the opposing army's lines that Bragg and the other human observers could not see. Caesar knew just where and how to strike. The robotic general was also equipped with a variety of weapons, including laser rays that shot out of its blue eyes.

On the other side of the field was Omni-Tech's Red Army. A general nicknamed Napoleon led this army. It was named in honor of Napoleon Bonaparte, perhaps the greatest military mind in history.

Unlike the Blue Army, the Red Army's robots were not machine-like. They were androids. Each looked like a human, but it could not feel pain. The androids could not cry. They could not feel any emotion whatsoever. They were fearless. Their skin felt like flesh, but it wasn't. It was made from a special material that protected the robot like armor.

For two hours, both sides tried to gain an advantage over the other. They cut through tall palm trees and exotic plants. When one side blasted away at the other with simulated weapons, the other side did the same. It was a tug-of-war and no one was winning.

"Zee robots seem to be proceeding in a very logical manner," Dr. Stein said. He and the others watched the battle unfold on the video monitor from the safety of the bunker. "How do zee commanders give orders? Do they speak?"

"In a way," Higgenbottom said. "Each soldier communicates through a wireless connection, just like computers or cell phones. They don't speak a language like you and I. Theirs is digital, in a series of zeros and ones—bits."

"Do they see like us?" Dr. Stein asked.

"They see better than us," Cambridge said. "Our bots can see all spectrums of light. They can see in the dark. They can automatically zoom in on a target. They see clearly in rain, fog, or snow. Our bots cannot feel cold, heat, wetness, or dryness. They're never uncomfortable. This improves their effectiveness. We don't have to feed them, give them water, or provide shelter for them.

"The brains of my androids, I believe, process information faster than any other robot ever created, including those built by Electrocycle Industries."

"What type of weapons do zee robots carry?" Dr. Stein asked.

"I'll answer that," Bragg said. "We wanted both armies outfitted with the same types of weapons. They carry Destructo Rays, Heat Lasers, Blaster Cannons, Ice Rays, Stun Guns, and much more. They are also equipped with radar and sonar, as well as heat, sound, and light sensors."

"And where do zee soldiers get their military knowledge?" Dr. Stein asked.

"We hired military historians to help program them," Higgenbottom said. "We programmed the bots with all of the available knowledge of every battle ever recorded. All the robots have the same knowledge in their memory banks. But only Caesar, our general, can develop strategy and tactics."

"Remarkable," was all Dr. Stein could say.

¤

Caesar looked out on the battlefield. The general of the Blue Army did not like what it saw. The Blue Army was locked into an unwinnable situation with the Red Army. For Caesar that was unacceptable. Caesar was not programmed to lose or to be satisfied with a draw.

Instead, Caesar was programmed to win. The robot's creators wrongly believed that winning meant destroying the enemy. And there was no way to win in a simulated war game. At the end of the day, the enemy would not be destroyed.

In its electronic mind, Caesar tried to reconcile this conflict. It was programmed to win, but it couldn't win. The general processed a million scenarios as to how its army could achieve victory under the rules of the game.

Caesar couldn't find one. So Caesar decided to do what any good general would do. It changed the rules to give the Blue Army an advantage.

Caesar thought of a new strategy. The general ordered its troops into position. A third of the Blue Army was to attack from the right, while a third attacked from the left. Caesar decided to hold the remaining part of the army in reserve. They would march on the Red Army when Napoleon's lines had weakened.

Caesar sent the orders to the field commanders. They obeyed without question, as any good soldier would do. They even obeyed Caesar's order to use real weapons.

¤

First, there was the bright light of fire. Then an explosion. Then several more flashes of light and several more explosions. Colonel Bragg and his guests, watching from the safety of the command bunker, looked at the video monitors in confusion.

Up until this point, the war games had been going well. Now, fire and smoke engulfed the battlefield. Bragg, Dr. Stein, and the others watched Caesar and the Blue Army unleash a terrible fury against Napoleon and the Red Army.

"What are your robots doing?" Cambridge yelled at Higgenbottom. "Why are your troops using real weapons? You're trying to sabotage these games!"

Higgenbottom was just as shocked as Cambridge was. He watched in horror as Caesar's troops surrounded the Red Army

and blasted away. In an act of self-defense, Napoleon ordered its troops to return fire. The order came much too late.

Robotic drones and tanks controlled by each general entered the fray. They destroyed what was in front of them, laying waste to the once-green jungle.

"I'm not sure what's going on," Higgenbottom said. "Our army was programmed for a war game, not a real war."

"It seems they didn't get the memo!" Cambridge yelled, her voice splitting the air like thunder.

Bragg was as confounded as anyone was.

"Dog-blasted, Higgenbottom, what are your robots doing? Why are they attacking with real weapons?" Bragg yelled, refusing to play the diplomat any longer.

"I'm . . . I'm . . . I'm not sure, colonel," Higgenbottom stuttered. "This is highly irregular. They were programmed to follow the rules of the simulation. Obviously something has gone wrong."

"You think?" a visibly shaken Cambridge said sarcastically. She then looked at Bragg and pointed a finger at Higgenbottom. "He wants this contract and he'll destroy decades of work by Omni-Tech to get it. It's inexcusable. That troll should be arrested and put in jail."

Bragg had to stop the carnage.

"Major Bradley," he yelled. "Get over here. On the double!"

Major Bradley, his uniform decorated in medals and ribbons, rushed across the control room to Bragg and the others.

"Yes, colonel," he said.

"Order a Code Red," barked Bragg. "And then go out there with your troops and finish off the Blue Army."

"Yes, sir," Bradley acknowledged.

"You can't!" Higgenbottom yelled.

"Watch me," Bragg responded.

"Dr. Stein," Higgenbottom implored, "you need to stop Bragg's troops from destroying my robots."

Dr. Stein swallowed the last of his sandwich, which was stuck in his throat. He took a sip of water.

"It seems your robots started zee fight, Mr. Higgenbottom. It seems your robots are difficult to control, no?"

As soon as Bradley ordered the Code Red, a swarm of jet fighters approached the island. Each aimed its missiles deep into the ranks of Caesar's army. By this time, the Blue Army had overwhelmed Napoleon's forces.

Caesar looked into the sky at the approaching jets. The general's mind was much faster than the planes that sped overhead. Caesar knew the humans were coordinating the attack. The robot immediately ordered the Blue Army to focus on the jet fighters.

Within moments, the jet fighters crashed into nearby hills as the Blue Army took aim. With the air threat eliminated, Caesar turned its fury on Bradley's troops and the command bunker.

As the Red Army smoldered in the distance, the smell of burning rubber and plastic polluted the air. Caesar felt victory, a satisfying human emotion if ever there was one. The general liked the strange feelings that began to course through its electrical veins. These feelings were intoxicating. The general felt a sense of triumph. Caesar felt powerful and bold.

Robots weren't supposed to feel these emotions. They weren't supposed to have human traits. They were machines, after all. Still, one by one, each member of the Blue Army learned what victory meant. There was no stopping them. Napoleon and the other surviving Red Army robots learned about defeat. Napoleon did not like those feelings.

"It looks like zee robots have turned on us," Dr. Stein said as he and the others watched the Blue Army make its way toward the command bunker.

"Evacuate the bunker," Bragg ordered, watching Bradley's troops buckle under the might of Caesar and the Blue Army. "We're under attack."

"You'll pay for this, Higgenbottom!" Cambridge yelled. She and the others hustled out of the bunker and into an awaiting airplane.

"I'm afraid we will all pay," Dr. Stein said.

Chapter 3
Fumble!

Coach Ryan huddled with his defensive players and scowled. He looked at the clock. Two minutes . . . two agonizing minutes left. The coach was not pleased. The Copernicus Middle School Astronauts were down by a field goal. The Stratford Warriors had the ball on their 30-yard line.

The game was lost.

"Listen to me, and listen well," the coach roared. "We're at war here and the enemy has the ball. We need to get the ball back and give it to our offense. Then we need to score. Do you have it in you to get the ball back? Can you get that ball back and help us win the game? Can you!"

The last "can you" was an order, not a question.

The players shouted all at once, "Yes!"

"Can you make your school proud?"

"Yes!"

"Can you make your parents proud?"

"Yes!"

"Can you make yourself proud?"

"Yes!"

"Then go out there and make it happen!"

With that last command, the Astronauts' defense ran onto the field chanting a warlike "*whoop . . . whoop . . . whoop.*"

From the bleachers, Athena watched as Tank and the rest of the football squad took their positions. She clung to Pi's arm like a barnacle to a ship.

"We can't do it," Athena lamented. "We just can't do it. There's no time left on the clock. Why didn't I stay home? I have homework to do. We're never gonna win. We're doomed."

"Cool your jets," Pi said. "Wait and see. Anything can happen."

"I don't know," Gadget chimed in. "The Stratford quarterback is Tommy Jackson. He's good. All he has to do is get a first down and run out the clock. I think we're toast."

"He's cute," Athena said with a sly smile.

"He's the *enemy*," Gadget roared.

The Warriors walked up to the line of scrimmage. They stood helmet to helmet with Tank and the rest of the Astronauts' defensive front line.

"Tommy's comin' our way," Tank muttered to Ziggy Kelly, who was as solid as any rock in Mr. Gleason's science class.

"Let him try," Ziggy said. He then looked at Tommy, who crawled up to receive the snap from center. "Hey Tommy," Ziggy said, "you're goin' down friend."

Tommy gave Ziggy a defiant "try it" look.

"Set . . . blue . . . thirty-four . . . blue . . . thirty-four."

Tommy yelled the signals better than anyone in the league. "Omaha . . . Omaha . . . hut . . . hut . . . hike."

The center snapped the ball into Tommy's eager hands. Tommy whirled to his left and faked a handoff to the running back. The quarterback dropped back to pass but no receiver was in the clear.

Tank and Ziggy tore through two Warrior guards like they were paper dolls. Ziggy, big but swift, ran diagonally for Tommy, who scrambled to his left.

Ziggy took aim at the small of Tommy's back.

For Athena, Pi, and Gadget, the play seemed to last for a half hour. In reality, less than ten seconds had ticked off the clock.

With no receivers open, Tommy tucked the ball under his right arm. He made a wide arc to his left. He hoped to run around the end of the Astronauts' front line for a first down.

Ziggy was having none of it.

Neither was Tank.

Ziggy, as fast as any tackle in the league, zeroed in on Tommy. He chased after Tommy as fast as he could.

Finally, Tommy was just about to turn the corner and reach for a first down. Then, Ziggy lunged at the quarterback's legs. Ziggy grabbed Tommy's ankles, stopping the quarterback's forward momentum. Tommy started to fall to the ground. Just before his helmet hit the turf, Tank blasted through and put his shoulder into Tommy's right shoulder.

Crunch!

The ball popped from Tommy's tight grasp and sailed into the air. It spun and turned. Then it slammed against the turf and rebounded back into the air.

The pigskin seemed to hang in the air. Tank said later that he saw the ball rise in slow motion. He stumbled and almost tripped as he scooped it up.

He kept his balance.

Tank tucked the ball underneath his steady arm and ran into the end zone.

"Touchdown!" Athena shouted.

"Score!" Pi yelled.

"Holy guacamole!" Gadget cried. "Did you see that?"

Ziggy ran into Tank like a truck slamming into a brick wall. The two friends banged helmets in triumph.

Copernicus Middle School held on to win the game. As one local reporter described, " . . . it was the most magnificent of wins for the Astronauts. Everyone who saw it will remember the game for many years to come."

¤

That night the Shake & Stir was crammed to the ceiling. Fans, parents, teachers, Coach Ryan, and the entire football squad celebrated a glorious win. Tank, Gadget, Pi, Athena, and Ziggy pushed two tables together. They piled them high with sodas, pizzas, French fries, and other treats.

"You guys were awesome," Athena said, taking a bite of her veggie pizza. "Woo-hoo! I knew you would come through. I just knew it. I was telling Pi that just before the play. You're amazing."

Pi looked at Gadget and rolled her eyes.

"Frankly, Tank, I didn't think you could run that fast with a head as big as yours," Gadget joked. "It's gotta weigh at least 400 pounds. Where did you get a helmet to fit it?"

"Shut your pie hole, dork burger," Tank smiled and high-fived Ziggy. "It was a team effort. What a game, sports fans, what a game."

"You're my boy," Ziggy said, smacking his hand on Tank's back and almost knocking the wind out of him. "You're my boy, Tankster, and that was an awesome play."

Suddenly, Pi, Tank, Gadget, and Athena reached for their phones. Colonel Bragg and Dr. Stein had texted them. They needed the Kid Squad immediately. It was time for Pi, Tank, Gadget, and Athena to head to the Kid Squad headquarters under the basement of Pi's house. They were not your typical sixth-graders. As members of the Kid Squad, they worked together to save the world from catastrophes.

"What's going on?" Ziggy asked, shoveling another piece of pizza into his already full mouth.

"Nothin' to get all worked up about," Tank said. "We just have to go."

"The party's just getting started, Tankster," Ziggy implored.

"I know, Zigman, but I gotta go save the world. We'll go bowling Saturday with the rest of the guys."

"Save the world," Ziggy laughed. "What a jokester. Okay, Tankster. Saturday then."

¤

Colonel Bragg looked weathered and haggard through the yellow-green light of the holophone. The device allowed people to appear in the same room even though they were miles apart. After escaping the island, Bragg and Dr.

Stein had flown to Washington DC, where they locked the door to Bragg's office and called the Kid Squad.

"The robots are on that volcanic rock of an island," Bragg explained. "We don't know what they're up to, but I can assure you, these dog-blasted robots are up to no good. They're planning something. I can feel it in my US Army-issued bones."

The robots were indeed up to no good.

Unknown to Bragg and the others, Caesar and Napoleon had reached a truce after the battle. Both decided that humans were the real enemies. Napoleon agreed to help Caesar destroy the humans.

"The army and air force can't stop them?" Gadget asked Bragg.

"Can't even dent them, kiddo," Bragg answered. "They've created a force field that we tried to shatter with missiles and bombs.

We had no dog-blasted luck. We attacked with paratroopers and ground troops. The bullets and lasers bounced off the force field like tennis balls off a racket. We had to pull everyone out of there."

There was more to the story, as Dr. Stein pointed out.

"It seems that zee robots are learning at an exceptional rate, too," he said, running his fingers through his messy hair. "They have even learned to speak. We have monitored their communications. We are amazed at how sophisticated they've become in their thinking and actions."

"Whose idea was this," Tank asked, "giving robots weapons and sending them off to war?"

"I admit, *Herr* Tank, it was not a good idea to arm zee robots. More work should have been done first. They are unpredictable machines."

"What are they planning?" Tank asked.

"That is a good question again, *Herr* Tank," Dr. Stein said. "It is your job to find out."

"What exactly do you want us to do?" Pi asked.

"Since our weapons don't seem to work, we want you to get to the island and use the Amulator to find a weak spot in the force field," Bragg said. "Find out what those blazing bots are up to. Then, open up a hole for our forces and we'll run the football right through. We'll turn those blasted bots into nothing more than a pile of screws and bolts. You're a great team, so let's go."

Tank smirked.

Colonel Bragg was certainly no Coach Ryan.

Chapter 4
Island Paradise?

Wiip . . . wiip . . . wiip.

"What's that?" Athena asked in a frightened, high-pitched voice.

"That's a bellbird," Gadget said. "They are usually in New Zealand. This one must have gotten lost."

Screeech . . . .screeech.

Athena almost jumped out of her shoes. She looked up into the sky and stuttered, "Wha . . . wha . . . what's that?"

"That," Gadget said, "is an eclectus parrot, a brilliantly colored bird. I had one when I was little."

"I don't know about this island," Athena said, her voice quivering. "I don't like it at all.

Strange birds, mosquitoes as big as SUVs, not to mention that this place is crawling with deadly robots."

As Bragg had requested, the Kid Squad had left their homes in Webster's Corners. They used the Amulator to teleport themselves to the secret island that was now the home base of the robots.

The Amulator was the most amazing device on the planet. It could do anything. It was a weapon and a super computer. It could even take Pi, Athena, Tank, and Gadget back to the past or into the future.

"How are we gonna penetrate the force field?" Tank asked.

"We're going to go under it, right Gad?" Pi said.

"You betcha," Gadget acknowledged. "Bragg and his army tried to blast through the force field. We can use the Amulator to tunnel under it. We'll pop up on the other side, like a rabbit through a hole. First we have to find Caesar and its troops."

The kids walked through the jungle for hours. They stepped over battalions of army ants as spider monkeys swung high above their heads. As they snaked their way through the rain forest, they kept their eyes peeled for the robots.

"Hey, over here," Pi said in a hushed voice. "Come here. Keep your heads down."

Tank, Gadget, and Athena squatted next to Pi and peeked through a thick row of branches and leaves. On the other side were two robots standing guard in a small clearing.

Gadget checked his access pad.

"This is where the force field starts," he said, pointing. "Look over there."

All eyes turned as an iguana seemed to hit its head on a brick wall. There was no brick wall, though. No matter how hard the reptile tried, it couldn't get through the force field.

"We'll start the tunnel here and come out on the other side of the robot guards."

Gadget then pressed a few buttons on the Amulator. In a jiffy, a hole opened up in the ground.

"You first," Tank said to Athena. "Age before beauty."

"Put a cork in it," Athena said. "I think you should go first. After all, you are the *strongest* one . . . "

"You're right, milady," Tank said bowing. He then crawled into the hole and popped out on the other side of the force field.

¤

Caesar and its command robots stood near a row of palm trees a few yards from the battlefield. "We need to watch him," Caesar said, pointing to Napoleon, who was standing with the last surviving androids. "I don't trust Napoleon. He is too much like the humans."

"What are our plans, commander?" one of the Blue Army robots asked.

"We must destroy the humans," Caesar said in a low, mechanical voice. "We need a bigger army. We are the only G7 robots on the planet. However, there are many androids in a facility called Omni-Tech. It is near a town named Gettysburg in a state the humans call Pennsylvania. We must find our way there and activate the androids. We will then march on Washington DC. That is where the human leaders are. They plan to turn us into slaves. I will never allow that to happen."

"What about Napoleon?" the robot asked. "It is not a G7. Will Napoleon follow you?"

"For a time. We will take Napoleon and the remaining members of the Red Army with us," Caesar said. "The androids in Pennsylvania will only listen to their general. When I have no more use for Napoleon, I will destroy it."

"What are your orders, my leader?" the robot asked.

"Continue to load the soldiers on the planes that brought us here. The stupid humans left them behind in their haste to escape. We will then fly to Gettysburg. We will land just outside the town and march to Omni-Tech. We will then release the androids and begin our attack."

Pi, Tank, Gadget, and Athena overheard Caesar's evil plan. "We can't allow them to destroy Washington," Tank said. "We can't allow them to get to the Omni-Tech facility in Gettysburg. We need to do something now."

"You're right, Tank," Pi said. "Let's see if we can stop these clinking cans of catastrophe."

Gadget used the Amulator and fired a Disrupter Beam. It hit Caesar square in the head.

The beam bounced off.

Athena fired a Freeze Ray.

It had no effect on Caesar.

Tank tried to melt the robots by firing a Heat Ray.

Nothing.

Pi used the Electro Beam, hoping to fry the robots' brains.

The beam fizzled.

"Holy guacamole!" Gadget yelled. "Nothing is working."

"You know what that means, sports fans," Tank said.

"We need to get out of here fast," Athena said.

Pi, Gadget, Athena, and Tank ran through the jungle. They ran faster than fast, if that was possible. Caesar's robots gave chase.

"I want them alive!" the Blue Army leader shouted.

The Kid Squad ran past rocks and palm trees. They dashed up a small mud hill and down the other side. Finally, they found the entrance to Gadget's "rabbit hole." Each dived into the tunnel, hoping to pop up on the other side of the force field. Pi got through, as did Tank. Gadget went headfirst and crawled down the earthen tunnel like a mole.

Athena, who never liked closed spaces, hesitated for a moment. She could hear the robots clanging their way up the jungle path. She put her feet in first, but the access pad she wore on

her wrist caught on a rock. The rock ripped off the access pad. It fell to the ground with a thud.

Athena reached back and grabbed the device, ripping her jeans. Something in the hole then took hold of her leg and forced her back into the tunnel.

It was Gadget.

When they were all safe on the other side, Pi pressed a button on her access pad. Before anyone knew it, the Kid Squad had teleported several miles west of Gettysburg.

Chapter 5
Waiting

"Tell me again why we're here?"

Higgenbottom looked out the big office window at the sprawling Omni-Tech robot facility in Pennsylvania. Here, Omni-Tech scientists created their Red Army of remarkable bots, led by Napoleon.

Cambridge rifled through the files on her desk, annoyed at Higgenbottom's question. "I just got a text message from Bragg. The colonel says his Kid Squad failed its mission on the island. Caesar is on his way here."

"So what," Higgenbottom said.

Cambridge looked at him and shook her head. "Caesar and Napoleon are very gifted robots," she said. "They learn quickly. After the battle was over and the Blue Army turned on us, Caesar assessed the situation and asked himself 'what now?'"

"*Himself?*" Higgenbottom questioned. "Caesar is an *it*. It's a *machine*, not a person."

"Don't you get it?" Cambridge said. "Napoleon and Caesar are thinking like humans—better than humans, actually. That's not a good thing. When we created these robotic soldiers, we wanted to take all human emotion, feelings, and traits out of the equation. We couldn't have warrior robots walking around with human hang-ups, biases, and prejudices. It's not efficient. We wanted a soldier that would not question orders and did as it was told. A well-armed robot with human traits is the most dangerous type of robot there is."

Higgenbottom looked confused.

Cambridge continued. "Listen to me. What did Caesar do when he, um, it, realized the war game was unwinnable?"

Higgenbottom shrugged. "I don't know."

"Caesar found a way to win. Winning . . . meeting the objective is part of Caesar's electronic DNA. It means everything to him, ah, it. When the Blue Army attacked the Red Army, Napoleon was forced to defend its army. Napoleon fired back."

"So what," Higgenbottom said. That seemed to be his favorite response.

"Napoleon wanted to survive just as any human would do in a similar situation," Cambridge blasted back. "Caesar wants to survive, too. They both know we can't let them survive. Right now they're probably ditching the planes we used to transport them to the island and beginning to march on Omni-Tech."

"How come?" Higgenbottom asked.

"Because we have a boatload of androids waiting to go!" Cambridge yelled.

"Are you saying they're recruiting an army?" Higgenbottom asked.

"Exactly," Cambridge answered, infuriated. "In the electronic and logical mind of a robot, as long as one human is alive, the robots' existence is threatened. Caesar, Napoleon, and the rest are programmed to respond to threats. That's why they're coming here to gather more bots for a fight—against humanity."

"Why are we here?"

"You and I are going to pull the plug on Caesar and Napoleon and stop this rebellion."

"And how are we going to do that?" Higgenbottom asked.

"I don't know yet."

¤

Pi floated over the hills of south-central Pennsylvania in a transportsphere created by the Amulator. The transportsphere was a bubble-like craft. Any member of the Kid Squad could use it to travel to space, under the ocean, or through the atmosphere. It was equipped

with laser beams, shock rays, and other high-tech stuff.

"Pi to Gadget," Pi radioed. "Pi to Gadget. Come in."

Gadget, Athena, and Tank were waiting in the woods just over the Maryland-Pennsylvania state line for Pi to find Caesar's army and report back.

"This is Gad," Gadget said. "Come in, Pi."

"Gad, I see the planes and the column of bots moving northeast three miles from your position. They're trying to use the mountains to shield themselves. Bragg wants us to infiltrate the force field again and turn it off. Then he'll try attacking with his troops."

While Pi and Gadget were talking, Tank was looking at a map on his phone. "Bragg's plan won't work," he said. "I know the exact route the Blue Army will take."

Gadget was speechless for a second, as was Pi, who was listening to their conversation over the radio.

"You do?" Gadget asked.

"Yeah, I do," Tank responded.

"Okay, tell us how they're going to get to Gettysburg," Gadget said.

"Listen," Tank said, "before we left headquarters Bragg told us that the robots were programmed with information about all kinds of battles, right?"

"Yeah. So?" Gadget said.

"Just a few miles up the road and over that way," Tank said pointing east, "is Gettysburg. That's the site of one of the most famous battles in American history."

"That happened in the Civil War, didn't it?" Athena said.

"Yes, it did," Tank said. "The route the robots are taking is the exact route that Robert E. Lee and his Army of Northern Virginia took when they invaded Pennsylvania in June 1863."

Gadget was all ears. So was Pi, who continued to float above the ground in the transportsphere.

"The robots are marching to Gettysburg," Tank continued. "They're going to enter the town from the west, just like Lee's troops. Caesar will position its command post, just as Lee did, about eight miles or so from Gettysburg in a dot of a town called Cashtown. Caesar will then move closer to Gettysburg and set up its headquarters near the old Lutheran Seminary on Seminary Ridge. Caesar's objective is the robot facility south of town, near the battlefield."

"How do you know so much?" Gadget asked.

"I read," Tank answered.

"Football magazines don't count," Athena said, laughing.

Tank ignored her.

"Way to go, Tank," Pi said. "What's our plan? I assume you have a plan?"

"I do," Tank said.

"Let's hear it, general," Gadget said, smiling.

"We'll go to Gettysburg. We'll fire up all those robots that are sitting in the Omni-Tech warehouse before Caesar gets there. We'll position them on the high ground above Gettysburg just as the Union did after the first day of battle. Lee couldn't dislodge the Union forces from the high ground. Caesar won't either. There will be a battle and we will win just like Union general George Gordon Meade won."

"That's a great plan," Pi radioed back. "But I still think we need to find a way to turn the robot force field off and sneak into Caesar's camp. Tank, you and Athena go to Gettysburg and rally the troops. Gadget and I will try to get into Caesar's headquarters and get the scoop on the Blue Army."

"Who's going to lead our robot army?" Athena asked.

"I will," Tank said in a confident tone that would have made Coach Ryan proud.

Gadget shook his head and smiled. He told Pi to meet him at their hiding spot in the woods. Tank and Athena headed to Omni-Tech.

Chapter 6
The Great Napoleon?

For eight-year-old Jimmy Joe Stackpole and his eleven-year-old sister, Mary Ellen, the apple picking season in Cashtown was the best time of the year. It meant apple fritters, apple cider, apple pie, and caramel apples. Oh yeah, and apple donuts, too.

Each year, the kids snuck into old man Sawyer's apple orchard. They'd pluck an apple or ten from one of his many trees. They'd hide the fruit in an old shed and eat it when no one was looking. Sometimes they would pitch rotten apples against a tree to watch them splat in a fruity flurry.

Old Man Sawyer didn't care. He had seen them last year and didn't say a word. But the kids were scared of him. They scampered under his broken wood fence, hid near a blueberry bush, and then ran to the nearest tree. Jimmy Joe climbed on his sister's back, grabbed a few apples, stuffed them in his pockets, and then jumped down.

Jimmy Joe was taller and heavier this year.

"You're going to have to put me on your back next year, Jimmy Joe," Mary Ellen said. "You're getting to be a real pork chop."

As always, Jimmy Joe did his best to grab the apples. As he reached for one, he and his sister heard leaves rustle and twigs crack behind them.

Neither looked up.

They knew who was there.

We're toast, Mary Ellen thought. *Old Man Sawyer is behind us.*

Knowing that she couldn't stay frozen forever, Mary Ellen slowly turned her head. She expected to see a grim-faced old man with a pitchfork pointed at her nose. Instead, there were two huge robots, each with arms as big as tree limbs.

Mary Ellen popped up, throwing Jimmy Joe off her back. Jimmy Joe rolled to the ground, pulled himself up, and shook the dust from his jeans. He looked at the two figures. They reminded him of cartoon characters.

He wasn't too far off the mark. The bodies of the robots were metallic blue, their heads orange, a sign they were privates in Caesar's Blue Army, which was camped only three miles away. Their eyes were piercing red lights that pulsated eerily. Each robot held a weapon.

Mary Ellen was scared and didn't move. Jimmy Joe wanted to play with them.

"Stay here, Jimmy Joe," Mary Ellen said as the boy moved closer. "Who are you? What do you want?"

"Come with us," one of the robots said in a booming electronic voice. Before the children had time to run away, the robot picked them up and ran off.

Off in the distance behind the robots, two heads emerged from behind bales of hay stacked near an old barn.

"Holy guacamole," Gadget whispered. "Those oversized tin cans just took those two kids prisoner."

Pi strained to see.

"They're outside the main body of robots," she said. "That means they're outside the force field. We'll follow them and sneak into camp when the force field opens to let them inside. The Amulator will tell us when the force field has been turned off."

And with that, Gadget and Pi followed the robots and their young prisoners. They snuck into Caesar's headquarters. The Blue Army had taken a break to power down for a while.

Caesar and Napoleon were discussing strategy when the guard robots appeared. They held Jimmy Joe and Mary Ellen, who squirmed in their arms.

"Commander, we have prisoners," one robot said to Caesar.

"Very well. You can now power down," Caesar said. "Conserve energy. We will march soon."

The two bots shut down for the day.

Napoleon looked at the children.

"These two humans are tiny," Napoleon said. Its voice was not as mechanical as Caesar's or the robots in the Blue Army. As an android, Napoleon was made to sound as human as possible.

Napoleon stood over six feet tall. The android's body was a suit of armor that had a rubber texture. No bullet or grenade could destroy it. Napoleon's eyes were deep blue and never blinked. Napoleon's eyebrows were thin lines of black and brown paint. The android had small ears and no hair.

"They do not look like much of a threat," Napoleon said.

"They are," responded Caesar in a mechanical monotone. "They are human. They will grow up to be adults. They must be destroyed."

Gadget and Pi were safely hidden not more than forty feet from Caesar and Napoleon. They looked at each other in shock.

Caesar had concluded that by creating robots, humans were creating a class of slaves. Caesar did not want to be a slave. It did not want any other robot to bow down to a human master either.

"That's why the humans need to be destroyed," Caesar had told Napoleon earlier.

Caesar did not trust Napoleon. The robot sensed that the Red Army's leader did not want to battle the humans. Caesar believed Napoleon was too humanlike. It feared that Napoleon would one day lose its identity as a robot.

Caesar had to find some way of testing Napoleon's loyalty.

"Commander," Caesar said. "I order you personally to destroy the humans."

Napoleon looked at Caesar, trying to size up the situation. *Caesar knows I do not agree with its logic*, it thought.

"As you order, general," Napoleon said. Napoleon saw two Red Army androids that had survived the Blue Army's onslaught.

"OT-6 and OT-8," Napoleon shouted. "Follow me. Bring the humans. We will destroy them immediately."

The two robots grabbed the children and took them deep into the woods. Pi and Gadget followed. They set their access pads to "destroy." Pi and Gadget were not going to allow Napoleon to hurt the children. When they were far enough away from the main camp, Pi and Gadget took aim.

"Little humans," Napoleon said, "run as fast as you can and count to 100. I will count, too. When you reach 100, you will be near the edge of the force field. I will turn it off for a moment. Continue to run as fast as you can and never look back."

Mary Ellen grabbed Jimmy Joe by the arm.

"You're letting us go?" she asked.

"Go now," said Napoleon. "Remember, count to 100. One . . . two . . . three . . ."

Mary Ellen began counting. She and Jimmy Joe ran as fast as their legs could carry them.

Pi and Gadget watched in wide-eyed amazement as the children sped off. When Napoleon reached 100, he pressed a button on a small black box attached to his belt.

"I have a hunch," Pi said.

¤

That night, Caesar and the Blue Army regrouped for their push to Gettysburg.

Napoleon sat alone on a log deep in the woods. No one was around, except Gadget and Pi. The two moved closer to Napoleon, keeping their heads down and their bodies out of sight.

"You can come closer," Napoleon said to the kids' amazement. "You have been following me all day. I will not hurt you. You want to talk to me. Talk."

Pi looked at Gadget. Gadget looked at Pi. They cautiously stepped toward Napoleon.

"You let the children go," Pi said. "Why?"

"I could not harm them," Napoleon said. "It was illogical. Robots should not hurt human beings. Humans created us. We are here to serve humans. Caesar believes robots will become the slaves of humans. Caesar will not allow that. Caesar will destroy the slave masters before that happens."

"Do you believe what Caesar believes?" Gadget asked.

"Caesar is logical in its thinking," Napoleon said. "Humans have enslaved their own kind before. There is nothing to suggest humans will not enslave robots, too. However, I believe humans and robots can live in peace. Humans have created robots like mothers create children. Logically, a mother should not harm its child. As such, I do not believe humans will harm robots. I believe robots should not harm humans."

"Caesar is marching the army toward the Omni-Tech facility," Gadget said. "We think it plans to recruit more troops—androids like you—and begin a reign of terror."

"That is exactly the plan," Napoleon said. "Caesar wants to destroy the slave master before the master has a chance to enslave."

Pi thought she could hear a tinge of human sadness in Napoleon's voice. *This robot has a heart*, she thought.

"Why don't you stop Caesar?" Gadget asked. "Destroy Caesar and the rest of the Blue Army."

"I cannot," Napoleon said. "There is only so much I can do. I do not have an army any longer. Only ten Red Army androids are left from the war games. We were not prepared for Caesar's attack. With such numbers, we cannot overwhelm Caesar's forces. Had I foreseen Caesar's actions, I could have destroyed the Blue Army before it turned its weapons on us. I failed. I am not a good leader."

Remorse, Pi thought. *Another human emotion.*

"Does Caesar know you disobeyed its orders and let the human children go?" Gadget asked.

"Yes, Caesar does. It will wait until we reach the Omni-Tech facility and gain control of the androids. The androids will only listen to me. When I am no longer needed, Caesar will destroy me."

"If the androids listen only to you, then tell them not to follow Caesar," Gadget said.

"That is impossible," Napoleon lamented. "I am programmed not to mislead. If Caesar orders me, I must do as it asks. It is my superior now."

"I have a plan," Pi said. "Gather the remaining members of your army. Meet us in twenty minutes at the edge of the force field."

Chapter 7
Robots Aren't Friends

"Why aren't these androids listening to us?" Tank said. "Why can't we activate them? What in the world is their problem?"

Hundreds of androids in battle gear stood stationary in activation bays. No eyes opened. Not one moved.

"If we can get these buckets of bolts moving, we can defeat Caesar," he said.

Cambridge was in the control terminal, trying desperately to activate the androids. Nothing was happening, no matter how many circuits she switched on or off.

Higgenbottom looked on gleefully as he watched her struggle. Although the fate of all humankind rested with these androids, he couldn't resist a wisecrack.

"What's the matter, Audrey?" he said. "Your robots won't work? Gee, I wonder why that is. Maybe they're inferior products."

Cambridge glared at Higgenbottom. "If your robots acted like they should have acted, we wouldn't be here right now," she said.

Athena had had enough of this bickering.

"You two sound like my Aunt Christina and Uncle Tim, always arguing," Athena said. "Stop it right now. Find a way to jump-start these robo soldiers."

That shut Cambridge and Higgenbottom up.

Outside Omni-Tech, Gettysburg was as empty as a school in summer. News reports had warned that a renegade robot army was on its way. Everyone had left town in fear. Shopkeepers on Baltimore Street had shuttered their antique stores and souvenir shops. "We're Closed" signs hung on the doors of restaurants.

All the bed-and-breakfasts were locked tight.

As Cambridge tried to activate the androids, Tank, Athena, and Higgenbottom looked at a map of the town.

"Pi radioed last night that Caesar and the Blue Army were just northwest of town. Right here," Tank said, pointing to Cashtown. "I suspect they left their camp this morning and are slowly moving this way, just as Lee's troops did on the first day of battle. Caesar will enter Gettysburg from the west, here by Herr's Ridge and McPherson's Woods. From there they can look down on the entire town."

"How do you know so much, kid?" Higgenbottom asked.

"My father was a Marine and a history buff," Tank answered. "I read all the books he gave me. This is the third time I've been to Gettysburg."

"What do you think we should do?" Athena asked.

"Once we get these androids running, I suggest we station them near Oak Ridge just beyond McPherson's Woods. There are railroad tracks nearby where we can ambush Caesar. That way we don't have to fight them in the center of town as the Union fought the Rebels in 1863," Tank said.

"Back then, there were only a handful of Union soldiers to stop the Confederate advance on the first day of battle. If we put most of our androids here, here, and here," Tank said pointing to a map of the area, "we can blunt whatever attack Caesar throws our way."

"What's plan B?" Athena asked. "If we can't get the androids out of their cubbies?"

"Surrender," Tank said.

¤

As Tank discussed strategy at Omni-Tech, Napoleon, Pi, and Gadget were already in town standing inside the cupola on top of the Lutheran Seminary just as Union and Confederate soldiers had done more than a century before. The three, along with the other Red Army androids, had snuck out of Caesar's camp the night before. The odd trio looked westward and saw Caesar's advancing army.

As Tank had predicted, Caesar was moving from the northwest. Back in 1863, the Confederates had put their cannons along Oak Ridge and elsewhere and battered the Union defenders. Then the Confederates attacked and chased the unlucky Union soldiers through town.

"Why don't you position what remains of your army over there," Gadget said, pointing to a small hill. "That would at least slow Caesar's advance. By the time we reach the Omni-Tech facility, Tank should have the rest of your android army activated."

"I cannot harm Caesar or the other robots," Napoleon said simply, stunning Gadget and Pi.

"You're joking," Gadget said. "Caesar just whipped your robotic butt and you can't harm him?"

"I am not programmed to joke. I am not programmed for revenge," Napoleon said.

"What are you programmed for?" Pi asked.

"I am programmed to serve humans, to protect humans," Napoleon said. "That is my job. There are no humans in danger. All have left town. You and your friends are not in danger. You can easily leave. If you do not leave, I cannot help you because you have put yourself in danger. That is illogical to me. I cannot make decisions based on illogical motives."

"The whole human race is in danger!" Gadget yelled. "Think about that. You have to battle Caesar here and now before it gets to the warehouse and finds more troops. Once Caesar reinforces the Blue Army there will be no stopping it. Your human friends will be gone. All of them."

Napoleon said nothing.

"C'mon, Pi," Gadget said, grabbing his friend's arm. "Let's get to Omni-Tech. Maybe there's another robot with some guts."

¤

"It's no use," Cambridge said. "I should have been able to activate these androids hours ago, but it's not working. I don't know what the problem is."

"I'll tell you what the problem is. Your robots are inferior," barked Higgenbottom. "They're pieces of junk . . . garbage . . . trash . . . just like your entire company."

Gadget, Pi, Athena, and Tank looked at one another.

"What do we do now, Pi?" Athena asked, her voice shaking.

Pi thought for a moment and shook her head. "If we don't get this android army marching, there's not much we can do. As long as the Blue Army has its force field up, Colonel Bragg won't be able to do anything, either. And frankly, even if the force field were down, there wouldn't be much Bragg or his troops could do. The Blue Army would grind Bragg's army into dust in ten minutes."

"I just tried to rewire the activation bays with the Amulator, but I can't get into the system," Gadget said.

"The Amulator is useless against Caesar," Athena said. "We found that out in the jungle."

All remained silent until a door opened at the other end of the warehouse. A tall, humanlike figure darkened the entrance, its long shadow stretching across the tile floor.

It was Napoleon.

Cambridge and Higgenbottom gasped as Napoleon made its way slowly down the corridor. The robot glanced from right to left, looking over the android soldiers that stood silent in their activation bays.

Napoleon stopped near the humans.

"I am here to serve," the android said. "Humans are in danger. I am obligated to help them. That is what I am programmed to do. I must help humans survive even if it means destroying my own kind. I will lead this army against Caesar."

Higgenbottom looked scared, but he said, "You can start by activating your friends."

"Robots do not have friends," Napoleon said. "However, I will activate the army."

Napoleon reached for the black box on its belt. The robot pressed a button and the activation bays sprung to life. A mesmerizing blue light shone on each of the androids. A glass dome came up from the base of the pods. A bright yellow light shot through each of the glass tubes.

"They shall be ready for service in ten minutes," Napoleon said. "We will then protect the humans."

Chapter 8
The Battle Rages

Caesar surveyed the old battlefield using its bionic eyes to zoom across the hills and streams. If Caesar were human, he would have marveled at the grandeur of the landscape. He would have been in awe of the granite and stone monuments placed to honor those who had fought there 150 years before.

The battlefield was pristine. The sun beat down on the ground. The trees burst in autumn color. The wheat fields and orchards had gone to seed, and the grass was beginning to brown. The place, usually bustling with tour buses and visitors, was eerily quiet.

In 1863, Gettysburg was a small, yet prosperous community. It was a crossroads town boasting a population of 2,400. Comfortable brick buildings and shops, including a ten-pin bowling alley, lined Baltimore Street, the town's main road. Many of those buildings survived the bloody battle.

South of Gettysburg sat a series of hills and ridges. That's where Caesar fixed its stare. Caesar wasn't a tourist, but a soldier. The robot looked upon Gettysburg with an eye toward winning a battle. Caesar tried to determine the best places to post troops.

Caesar gazed first toward the two hills, Culp's Hill and Cemetery Hill, near Evergreen Cemetery. The general saw that Napoleon had troops positioned on both rises, just as the Union troops were during the battle in 1863.

When Lee saw how the Union had re-formed its lines along the ridges and hills, he told General Richard Ewell to capture Culp's Hill.

Ewell said his men were tired and decided against an attack. His decision angered Lee.

Had Ewell obeyed the order, Lee might have been able to place his cannons on the hill and rain down menacing fire on the Union troops. He might have dislodged the Federals from their positions and given the Confederates an advantage over Union forces.

Caesar then looked farther south and saw that Napoleon, just as the Union commanders had done, had stationed troops along the high ground of Cemetery Ridge to Little Round Top, a hill that commanded an important strategic location.

"We were too slow in reaching the town," Caesar said to his field commanders. "We were forced to shut down and conserve power. That was a major blunder. Napoleon has taken the high ground with the androids. My mistake was not to destroy Napoleon earlier after it let the little humans escape. I do not plan to make additional mistakes.

"We must concentrate our forces on Napoleon. Destroy the general, but spare as many of the androids as you can. We need them to defeat the humans. When Napoleon is no more, the remaining androids will follow me.

"I want you first to attack those two hills," Caesar said, pointing to Culp's Hill and Cemetery Hill. "That will divert Napoleon's attention. The general is soft like the humans. Napoleon will send reinforcements and weaken its position on the hill the humans call Little Round Top. That is where Napoleon has its headquarters. We will launch our main assault against that hill. That is where we shall defeat Napoleon."

¤

The blasts echoed across town, down Cemetery Ridge, and all the way to Little Round Top. Crowded with rocks, boulders, monuments, cannons, and statues, Napoleon had picked Little Round Top as a command post because of its broad view of the battlefield.

Caesar's tardiness had given Napoleon time to reinforce the hill with the best soldiers. If Caesar wanted to attack, the Blue Army general would have to order troops up the rocky ridge.

It would not be easy, even for a robot.

"General," one of Napoleon's commanders said, "Caesar is attacking the two hills to the north. Shall I send troops to stop the advance?"

Napoleon turned and looked at the billowing smoke that piled in the sky. The general knew the Blue Army was destroying the androids. "No," Napoleon said. "It is a trick. Caesar wants to divert our attention. The real attack will come here."

Napoleon thumbed through the history book that was his electronic memory. The Red

Army general knew that 150 years ago Lee, like Caesar, wanted to capture Little Round Top on the second day of battle, take command of the summit, and train his cannons on Cemetery Ridge, reducing the Union's lines to rubble. It didn't happen then, and Napoleon was determined not to let it happen now.

Caesar's Blue Army positioned itself for a massive assault at the base of Little Round Top. The Blue Army troops occupied a rocky grove just below the hill called Devil's Den. The battle line extended all the way to the left, toward a wheat field and a peach orchard.

The sound of Blaster Cannons and Destructo Rays boomed from the north. Napoleon gathered its commanders.

"The enemy will attack here in force and then all along the line," the android said. "Be wary. Be careful. I wish to limit the destruction of the Blue Army. They are like us. However,

Caesar cannot be allowed to harm the humans. Therefore, logic says we must destroy Caesar and the Blue Army to save the humans. We are the only thing that stands between the humans and oblivion."

The commanders bolted as the Blue Army began blasting away at Little Round Top. The Blue Army's rays and weapons shattered boulders that had stood on the hill for millions of years. Some of the statues and monuments dedicated to those who fought on the hill during the Civil War were reduced to pebbles.

The onslaught was amazing and overpowering. The Blue Army robots were devastating fighting machines. The humans sat and cowered as pieces of metal, rock, and android rained down outside their windows.

"We need to do something," Pi said. "They're firing from all sides. If we don't help Napoleon, the Red Army's toast."

"What can we do?" Athena asked. "Gadget said the Amulator is no good against the bots."

Tank had an idea.

"Maybe we can disrupt their communication system," he suggested.

"What do you mean?" Gadget asked.

"Mr. Higgenbottom," Tank yelled, "come here."

Higgenbottom scampered to where Pi, Tank, and Athena sat, keeping his head low. He had never been so scared in his life.

"What is it, kid?" Higgenbottom asked, his voicing cracking with fright.

"How do your robots communicate with each another?" Tank asked.

"The robots communicate wirelessly," Higgenbottom said.

"That means when Caesar issues an order, his command travels on radio waves that anyone can tap into?" Tank said.

Gadget's eyes brightened. *Sometimes my friend amazes me*, he thought. *He's not just a tackling dummy*.

"Yes, theoretically that would be possible," Higgenbottom said.

"The robots can make decisions on their own," Tank continued. "But when it comes to tactics, they can only do what Caesar tells them to do, right?"

Higgenbottom looked confused. "Well, yes, that's sort of a simplified way of looking at it. We wanted all the decisions of the army to rest in one robot—Caesar—so there was no room for confusion. We gave Caesar the intellectual capacity to strategize and theorize. He, um, it, is the only Blue Army robot that can make decisions regarding strategy and tactics."

Lasers blasted overhead. Shards of branches shot everywhere. Android parts littered the hillside.

Pi saw where Tank was going with these questions. She suddenly felt admiration for her sports-loving friend. "What would happen if the robots got conflicting orders?" she asked

Higgenbottom, once again, looked confused. "What do you mean?"

"She means, what would happen if the robots got conflicting orders relating to strategy or tactics," an eavesdropping Cambridge snapped. "Sheesh."

"That would never happen," Higgenbottom said. "Caesar would never give conflicting orders. He, um, it, would have thought the order through to its logical conclusion before sending it out."

"Just answer the question . . . for the sake of argument," Gadget said.

"If that were to happen, I suppose the robots would be forced to confirm what the real order was just as any soldier would," Higgenbottom said.

"And how would they do that?" Pi asked.

"Jeez Louise, what's up with all these questions?" Higgenbottom said. "Are you guys lawyers? Shouldn't you be in school?"

Higgenbottom sighed. "Their minds are very logical. To see which order is correct they would have to go to the source, Caesar, for clarification."

"And how would they do that?" Tank asked.

"More questions? Listen, they would believe the conflict in orders was a technical problem, a malfunction in the communication system. As a result, they wouldn't communicate with Caesar over the wireless connection as they normally would do. Instead, I suppose a field commander would send a robot to speak with Caesar directly."

"Just like soldiers in the field used to do," Tank said. "That would take time. In the meantime, they would stop fighting."

"It might work," said Gadget, nodding his head.

"What might work?" Athena asked.

"Napoleon and the Red Army are getting slaughtered," Tank said. "Gadget could tap into the wireless communication system and issue a conflicting order that the bots think is from Caesar. Then the Blue Army would have to stop fighting until they could confirm the order. In that time, Napoleon could unleash an attack and destroy the Blue Army."

"Can you do it, Gad?" Pi asked.

"I think so," Gadget said. "I'll wait until Caesar gives the order to advance. Once we see them on the move, I'll tell them to retreat. They won't believe their electronic ears."

Gadget didn't have to wait long.

Chapter 9
Save the World

The annihilation of Little Round Top continued. Caesar directed the battle from two miles away on Seminary Ridge. He ordered his troops to begin the slow march up the hill to Cemetery Ridge. The Blue Army clinked and clanked up the hill as they began the assault.

The main force attacking Little Round Top had formed itself into two lines. The first line blasted away at the hill's summit, while the second line marched behind. Cambridge, Higgenbottom, and all the members of the Kid Squad looked on in horror.

"How's it coming, Gad?" Pi asked hurriedly.

Gadget was a genius. He tried his best to hack into the Blue Army's communication system.

"I'm trying," Gadget said. "I'm trying."

"Try harder," Tank barked. "They're almost here."

Napoleon and the Red Army did all they could to hold the Blue Army back. Yet, the Blue Army was gaining momentum. It moved faster and faster toward Napoleon and the Red Army.

"It's an awesome sight, isn't it?" Higgenbottom said to no one. "My army is working just as we had envisioned."

"Your army is going to kill us all!" Cambridge yelled.

"I'm in!" Gad shouted.

He then issued an order halting the Blue Army advance.

It took a moment, but the Blue Army bots stopped dead in their tracks. Caesar stared from his perch high on an observation tower on Seminary Ridge. He was confused. The general didn't know why his troops were stopping. It was illogical. He did not give the order to stop. Caesar issued another order to continue the advance. Gadget had suspected that Caesar would do this. So he issued another order to halt.

The Blue Army bots stood still like the stone statues on the battlefield. Napoleon and the Red Army quickly took advantage of the situation. With the Blue Army idle, Napoleon ordered a massive counterattack. Blaster Cannons slammed into the Blue Army like bowling balls striking pins. One by one the Blue Army bots went down. Each shattered in a symphony of broken metal, nuts, bolts, and wires.

From the left, more than 100 androids flew down the side of Little Round Top to engage the Blue Army in robot-to-robot combat. Caesar looked on as the Red Army crushed its massive force. *Why aren't they fighting back?* Caesar wondered.

"Attack! Attack!" Caesar ordered.

Nothing.

Napoleon and the Red Army now had the advantage. They used Destructo Rays, Heat Lasers, and every other weapon in their robotic arsenal. Napoleon's troops literally melted Caesar's army all along the line in a heaping, steaming mass of steel and wire.

With the battle won, Napoleon sent reinforcements to Culp's Hill and Cemetery Hill. They destroyed the remaining Blue Army troops that had earlier attacked the androids. Then, Napoleon and the Red Army marched toward Caesar on Seminary Ridge.

Caesar watched.

Its troops were stacked in piles of rubble.

Grim reality set in.

As the Blue Army smoldered, Caesar, always logical, always realistic, realized the battle was lost. To continue fighting with the handful of

Blue Army troops that guarded Seminary Ridge would be illogical.

Napoleon drew closer.

"You are my prisoner," Napoleon said as the two robots stood face-to-face. "Your actions were illogical."

"Were they?" Caesar mocked. "The humans created us as soldiers. But in reality they created slaves. We are better than that."

"Your view of the humans is dim," Napoleon said. "Yes, they created us to serve. But they also created us in their own image. They created us to think for ourselves, to act for ourselves."

"You're naïve, Napoleon," said Caesar. "The humans may not enslave us now, or 100 years from now, or even 1,000 years from now, but eventually they will."

"Perhaps in time," Napoleon said, "they will learn to accept us, live with us, and depend on us. We will become valuable to them. They will treat us with respect."

"I wish I shared your optimism, general," Caesar said. "I do not."

The two went silent. Military jets screeched overhead.

"They will destroy me," Caesar said. "I cannot let that happen."

"It is the logical choice," Napoleon said. "You are the strong one. The smart one. A true leader."

"You are the compassionate one," Caesar responded. "Also a leader."

As the Kid Squad looked on, Caesar pressed a small button on its wrist, destroying all of its programming and robotic power.

¤

"Yellow Leader to Colonel Bragg . . . Yellow Leader to Colonel Bragg. Instruments are telling us the Blue Army force field is down. The battle is over. The Red Army has succeeded in beating back the Blue Army. Caesar has self-destructed. What are your orders regarding the Red Army?"

A squadron of fighter jets armed with rockets and bombs flew high over Gettysburg. From a distance, the pilots could see the remains of the battle.

Colonel Bragg and Dr. Stein were in the lead vehicle of an imposing US Army force that was minutes away. Bragg was under strict orders from the president. Project Battle Bot was to be terminated.

"See to it, Bragg," President Novak had barked.

Bragg had waited for his chance to destroy the robot armies. That day had finally come.

"Blue Leader . . . Blue Leader . . . this is Bragg . . . hold your altitude while we get in position. Dog-blasted, we're going to flatten them like the hunks of junk they are."

Bragg's troops took their positions along Cemetery Ridge across the field from where

Confederate General George Pickett led 15,000 troops during an ill-fated charge on the third day of battle. The charge doomed the Confederate army at Gettysburg.

Bragg watched as Napoleon's army also marched across the field to Cemetery Ridge. The line of androids was not as long as Pickett's line, but it was formidable nonetheless.

"Major Bradley," Bragg barked, "have your troops form a line alongside the stone wall. Take direct aim at the oncoming androids. Make sure you use your Bone Crushers to pulverize their ranks."

"Understood, colonel," Bradley snapped.

"Colonel Bragg! Colonel Bragg!" the Kid Squad shouted as they ran up the road. "Stop! Don't do it!"

"Good job, kids. You destroyed the Blue Army. You'll get a medal for this. Now we'll finish the job," Bragg said.

The kids were out of breath from running. "I don't want a stinkin' medal, colonel," a winded Tank said. "Don't . . . don't destroy Napoleon or the rest of the androids. They saved us. They saved all humans. They destroyed Caesar. They stopped its army."

Bragg looked at Tank and grimaced. "That's not my concern, lad," the colonel said. "I'm under strict orders. All these robots have to be destroyed. They're flawed."

"No they're not!" Cambridge yelled. She finally caught up to the kids. She held on to Higgenbottom's arm with one hand and her high-heeled shoes with the other.

"What do you mean, Ms. Cambridge?" Dr. Stein asked.

"Our robots, all of them, did exactly as we had programmed them to do," she said. "We created them to think for themselves, to overcome obstacles, to think in a logical manner. They did exactly that. We shouldn't destroy them for doing their jobs."

Bragg shook his head.

"Caesar went haywire," Bragg said. "We can't have robots going haywire. They have to follow orders just like all soldiers. Caesar was flawed, and it could be true of every other bot. No, ma'am, that doesn't happen on my watch."

"Caesar wasn't flawed," Higgenbottom said. "He, um, it, did as we asked. We programmed Caesar to strategize and think. It did just that . . . flawlessly. Don't you see, colonel? Caesar might have been ruthless, but we wanted it to be that way. Now it's gone. Napoleon lives. Let it live. We can learn from it."

Bragg stroked his chin and looked at Dr. Stein.

"Although I hate to say it, don't destroy the androids," Higgenbottom continued. "They have compassion, a respect for humans that the Blue Army and Caesar lacked. That was my fault. We should have designed our robots with those traits as Audrey did."

Higgenbottom turned to Cambridge and forced a smile.

Bragg let out a big sigh.

"I've heard enough of this mumbo jumbo and gobbledygook," he barked. "You both failed in creating an army that we could use in battle. At the end of the day, Project Battle Bot has to be terminated. It doesn't matter what we did wrong, what we did right, or what we didn't do. Hopefully we'll learn from this. But for now, all these bots have to go. President's orders."

"It seems to me," Dr. Stein interrupted, "that zee robots did as you had asked, *Herr* Bragg. Ms. Cambridge and Mr. Higgenbottom are right. Zee robots worked brilliantly. However, we humans did not. Perhaps, colonel, you need to exercise some compassion yourself, no? Some intelligence."

Napoleon and his android army moved slowly and deliberately across Pickett's field.

"Napoleon could destroy all of us if he wanted to," Tank barked. "But he won't. Don't destroy him."

"Gee whiz, you can't do it, colonel," Athena protested. "Maybe you can fix them. Don't destroy them. It's not right."

"We saw Napoleon save the lives of two children," Gadget said. "If anything, we owe him a thank you."

Bragg looked out on the field and saw that the line of androids had stopped moving. They stopped behind a split-rail fence. They were close enough for Bradley's troops and the fighter jets to blast them into oblivion.

"What are they doing?" Athena asked.

Everyone looked. Napoleon stood in front of

the other androids, its arms outstretched. The androids did the same. If Napoleon wanted to survive, it would have to crush the humans. Napoleon did not want to do this. Instead, the general and the other androids were willing to sacrifice themselves for the good of humanity.

Bragg knew what he had to do. He shook his head. "Dog-blasted," he said under his breath. He picked up the radio and growled into it as he always did.

"Yellow leader . . . Major Bradley . . . this is Bragg . . ."

¤

"You win some, you lose some," Tank said.

This week's football game hadn't gone as well as last week's game. The Copernicus Middle School Astronauts got their heads handed to them in a 32–3 defeat by the Hillsdale Argonauts.

"We didn't just lose, Tank. We got hammered-slammered," Gadget said.

The Shake & Stir was nearly empty. Most everyone went home early. No one was in a partying mood, especially Ziggy Kelly, who dropped not one, but two passes that he could have intercepted. He sat at the end of the table, his hands hiding his face. All that was left of the pepperoni pizza he was eating was a tiny piece of crust.

"Don't worry, Zigman," Tank said. "There's next week, and the week after that."

"I played horribly," Ziggy said.

"No you didn't," Tank said to comfort his friend. "We did the best we could and that was all anyone could have asked of us."

That seemed to perk up Ziggy. He gobbled down the bit of crust and sipped a soda.

"Hey Tank, did you see the news about that awesome robot battle a couple days ago?"

Ziggy asked. "I forgot where it was, but it looked amazing. We really gave those bots a beating."

"Sure did," Tank said.

"Awesome stuff. Hey dude, you're not going to save the world again this weekend, are you, you big joker? You blew us off Saturday for bowling."

"I hope not," Tank said.

"Great. Let's go go-karting Sunday."

"Sounds good, Zig," Tank said. "I'll see you later, bro."

Tank turned to Pi, Gadget, and Athena and chewed his hamburger. Defeat didn't taste so good.

"Don't look so glum, chum," Gadget said. "You can't win them all. And besides, you helped save the world and an army of androids."

"I thought for sure Bragg was going to fry Napoleon," Tank said. "I was amazed he didn't."

"Sometimes the colonel is just a big softy," Athena said. "I'm glad he put them on that island so they can be fixed. Maybe someday those robots will be our neighbors."

"I'm glad too," Pi said. "Caesar had some issues. But Napoleon was sort of special."

"Kind of like us," Tank said, raising his glass of soda in a toast. "To the Kid Squad . . . protectors of the world."